Rock-a-bye

LIANA BROOKS

OTHER WORKS

ALL I WANT FOR CHRISTMAS

All I Want For Christmas Is A Reaper
All I Want For Christmas Is A Werewolf

FLEET OF MALIK

Bodies In Motion
Change of Momentum

HEROES AND VILLAINS

Even Villains Fall In Love
Even Villains Go To The Movies
Even Villains Have Interns
Even Villains Play The Hero (books 1 – 3 omnibus)
The Polar Terror

TIME AND SHADOWS

The Day Before
Convergence Point
Decoherence

SHORTER WORKS

Fey Lights
Prime Sensations
Darkness and Good

Find other works by the author at
www.lianabrooks.com

Rock-a-bye

INKLET #69

LIANA BROOKS

Inkprint PRESS

www.inkprintpress.com

Print ISBN: 978-1-925825-76-3
eBook ISBN: 9798201332716

www.inkprintpress.com

National Library of Australia Cataloguing-in-Publication Data
Brooks, Liana 1983 –
Rock-a-bye
52 p.
ISBN: 978-1-925825-76-3
Inkprint Press, Canberra, Australia
1. Fiction—Crime 2. Fiction—Short Stories

First Print Edition: November 2021
Cover photo © Khusen Rustamov via Pixabay
Cover design © Inkprint Press
Interior art © Amy Laurens

ROCK-A-BYE

"R OCK-A-BYE, BABY, ROCK-A-BYE."

It wasn't the worst house in Denver. The roof held shape, more or less. The shared wall of the rowhouses weren't up to code, but they were up. The neighborhood wasn't a an urban blight as much as it was an urban study in depression. This is where people came when everything was over.

When you lost your job but were too old to find another.

When you were sick and the medicine kept being too much to afford.

When you were a bright kid but you couldn't afford books for school, or college, and you married for the steady paycheck only to have the bastard leave you when the baby was sick, you wound up here. Between the rehabilitated crack addicts, the sex offenders, and the pensioners raising grandkids.

There was an apologetic knock on the door downstairs, the rhythmic equivalent of someone clearing their throat and making tentative eye contact while hoping no would actually make eye contact in return.

Tucking the blanket under the sleeping baby's chin, I went downstairs, thirteen slabs of rotting wood held together by faded carpet and prayers— although possibly not prayers to any god the Christians want to talk about.

Bolts slid out with a tick, and a thunk, and a crick, and a slish because the chain lock, heavy and old, stayed in place.

The door was something new, something I'd bought and installed myself, just like the windows in the front room and the ceiling between the living room and the upstairs bedroom that had rotted out before I moved in.

"Yes?"

"It's... a thing." The voice out in the darkness sounded male and elderly. "Neighbor said you do this sort of thing, maybe?" A folded piece of paper was shoved into the crack between my space and his; it smelled of bitter marijuana and anger and all it held was a name written in shaky letters.

"Got it." I pinched the paper without touching the client and pulled away.

"Do you—"

"No."

"I can—"

"Pass."

"Oh—"

The door slid closed. Rattle. Slish. Crick. Thunk. Tick.

The name had been working its way to my door for days. There was no magic to it. Currents of despair and the driving winds of desperation had knocked the name off its perch, the whispered name of a predator looking for young girls. The name of someone who filled this place with a suffocating darkness even the dying wouldn't accept.

Now the name was in my hands.

Despair had brought me here, led me by the hand until I sat among the broken. Despair had taken my name, my pride, my job—but somehow there was still work to do.

From the closet I pulled a candle and some wedge-heeled shoes. Not for magic; if there were gods, they prayed to me, not the other way around. The candle was for a much more practical purpose.

The wick caught flame quickly, and the name became ash in the fire. Ash that would feed the tree in my tiny garden.

Never heard of him, officer.

No one came here, officer.

He must be mistaken, officer.

The shoes fit comfortably. My long legs arched, tan and smooth, above them. The short skirt I wore because the air conditioning had never worked was good enough. The top was, perhaps, a little too loose and mature, but the pink fabric was light as a breath and just as see-through in the streetlights.

Tick. Thunk. Crick. Slish. Rattle.

The door opened.

Thunk.

The deadbolt fell back into place.

A cigarette would have been nice. Something to hold and burn against the darkness. But tonight there were only stars, a withering moon, and me walking up hill to the canal.

Down the hill was the pit, row-homes and apartments squished together, huddled masses.

Up the hill was the suburbs, the McMansions and tiny palaces earned from abusing low-level employees forty hours a week.

The canal ran between us, uncaring and filthy. There was an old jogging path there, littered with the more disposable forms of entertainment and overgrown. The poor didn't care, and the suburbanites never went here.

Streetlights were spread out every ten meters or so, casting pools of sickly yellow light. Not much, but what more did addicts need? Why spare the expense for people who were trying to hide their activities anyway?

A breeze ran past carrying the scent of the fish-choked canal, rancid beer, human sweat, and a maddening hunger. It was that kind of night, filled with wayward thoughts and grand ambitions.

Overhead a streetlight flickered and died.

Footsteps shuffled behind me as I walked past.

I moved faster.

The footsteps followed.

"Where you going, pretty girl?"

"Out for a walk. Couldn't sleep."

"Walk with me, pretty girl."

"I'm fine, thanks."

A rough hand closed around my arm. No pink fabric in the world was going to save me. "What's the hurry, pretty girl?" Yellow light showed a craggy face and a three-day beard that smelled of stale cooking grease.

"Let go."

"We're just talking, pretty girl." One hand pushed me back to the fence, the other went lower, searching for a belt buckle.

"Let go of me!"

"I will, soon enough." The belt buckle clinked as it fell. Clink. Zip. And the hushed crush of cloth falling.

A cold hand hit my bare thigh.

"Please. Please don't. I haven't—I don't want…"

The man laughed as his hand moved higher. "You wearing panties, pretty girl?"

When people are attacked, flight and fight are never the first response. Freezing is. The terrifying, will-destroying moment when your mind is so stunned you can't move.

Predators expect it. They know that moment is all they need.

In the frozen moment, where vision blurred and I collapsed back, shoulder blades bruising against the fence, I struck.

Face smashing into face.
Knee driving upward.

Knife catching the neck and three-day beard.

Tonk. Crunch. Slit.

The man dropped to his knees, clutching his throat.

A kick and he tumbled back into the fetid waters of the canal for the crawfish to devour.

Should have cleaned my knife first, but oh well, home wasn't so far away. The thin point slid back into the scabbard on the high waist of my tiny skirt.

The walk home was pleasant.

Thunk.

The door opened.

Tick. Thunk. Crick. Slish. Rattle.

The world was locked out again.

"Momma." Daniel sat at the top of the stairs, chubby fists wrapped around the iron of the railing. "Did you go out?"

"Oh, love, just for a moment. Mommy had some work by the water."

He sighed heavily for a boy so young.

"Go to sleep, love. Mommy will be here when the morning comes."

A light tread on the stairs. A swish of the door closing upstairs. A creak of the old bed as someone climbed in to sleep under the window.

And from upstairs the sound of a young voice softly singing, "Rock-a-bye, baby, rock-a-bye."

THE MAKING OF
ROCK-A-BYE

As a teen, I lived in a row house in a poorer neighborhood on the outskirts of Denver, Colorado. Despite being a larger city, Denver really wasn't that big (or didn't seem to be after living in Chicago). The house was poorly made, with leaking pipes and paper-thin walls between dwellings. There were no fire walls, no air conditioning, no privacy.

It was the kind of place you live in because you can't afford anything better, but you are desperately hoping that you'll one day escape. A step up from an apartment, but for most of the inhabitants it was as far as they were going to get away from the apartments.

There was a nearby walking path and a canal that divided the low income side of town from the "We can afford a mortgage!" side of town. I used to walk the dog there at night, listening to the crickets and looking in the lights from all the windows, each one a little shadow box of humanity showcasing one person's frail life.

For all the misery, all the tears and pain that were caught in that place, nothing too terrible ever happened there. But sometimes we wondered if it should.

CHANGE OF MOMENTUM: CHAPTER ONE

THE HYPERTRAM FROM RYUN to Kytan was running three minutes late, a silver-blue moonbeam racing across the golden desert. It was one of the little inefficiencies that made Malcolm Long hate ground travel. That and the other passengers, of course.

Waving off an offer of food from the refreshment cart, he settled into a seat on the port side of the tram and bullishly stared out the window as they rushed across the barren rock between the city-states.

High overhead, a shining Koenig-1-11 caught the sunlight as it turned for a landing in Dreyun to the north.

Long's lips twitched into a frown as he pulled out his ever-present palm pad to take notes. The one-elevens were supposed to be phased out by now. Blue Sky Air Transport had been sold off six weeks ago to Lethe, and Lethe was replacing the one-elevens with the Koenig-360, a plane with a fabulous interior and fuel consumption that made him wince.

He assumed that was why Lethe had contacted his offices two days ago to request this meeting. They were paying for his travel, and had offered a consulting fee that was generous without being obscene.

The whole set-up made the hair on the back of his neck stand up.

Senior engineers at small research firms did not generally get attention like this. Especially since he hadn't published anything in over a year. His team had been busy, and he'd been juggling too many projects to finish anything of substance.

If this was about the Koenig-360s, he could handle the matter in a couple of weeks. If it wasn't...

An old fear clawed up his throat.

For a moment the crowded tram was silent, devoid of oxygen, cold as the dark between stars. Memories of pain and rage threatened to destroy him. His heart raced as he fought the fear. Pulled it under. Drowned it in the memories of today.

That had been another life.

Another name.

A time of power and cruelty—because the two always went hand in hand. But it was the past. He'd left the islands and there was no way Lethe could know who he had been.

Lips twitching into a grim smile, he checked his watch as the rocks gave way to the cultivated terraces of Kytan. Red rock formations ringed what were laughably called terraformed plateaus, bordered first with grain crops dividing the desert from the cultivated countryside, and then the land rippled inward past pools of pale pink water lilies, and into a sea of blue-green iridescent irises that sparkled like a dragonfly's wing.

Kytan was famous for the blooms that appeared for six weeks during the height of the Descent wedding season. Right now, the city-state was overflowing with tourists who wanted to wander the parks and young couples taking engagement photos for next summer.

The tram went straight to the hanging gardens hiding the terraced buildings at the heart of the city. The air was cooler there under the shade of the vines, effervescent with the scent of falling water, and the crowd hurried past him to catch the city transports while he walked, briefcase in hand, along a stream-lined road.

The artisinal waterway was filled with silvery-blue fish that swam through the sun-dappled water against the current flowing down from the step pyramids at the city center.

The original home of the Imperial Governor of Malik IV, designed to match the legendary summer palace of Emperor Insei Qui the Third, the pyramids in the center of the city were an architectural wonder, covered in towering waterfalls and fronds and vines of greenery. Great stone mountains built in the desert plain and covered with a deep green jungle, with flowers of brilliant white and pink burning along the branches like captured stars. The whole city sparkled like the dead emperor's scepter, exactly as the first arrivals from the old Empire had hoped.

"A thousand years of freedom and still we bow," Long murmured to himself. He couldn't remember the rest of the poem now, but he remembered when he'd first heard it, in the halls at school spoken by a girl who'd both captivated and challenged him.

She would have appreciated the architecture of Kytan. Probably had the opportunity to, considering her family and wealth.

Or perhaps not.

With the powerful families on the first continent, it all depended on who you knew and who you were allied with.

The Longs were a small family with no allies, unless his mother's book club friends counted, which he personally didn't feel they needed to. A family name, the right genes, a pittance of an inheritance, and an acre of land somewhere out in the wilds between city-states. It had been enough to get his family off the islands along the edge of the second continent and earn him a scholarship to the most prestigious university, but it wouldn't keep him alive if the Lethes wanted him dead. Especially not here in their capital city.

"I suppose I should have asked for a bodyguard," he muttered to himself. One of the lab interns had the height and reach to be a good shield—but also the personality of a frightened rabbit, which might have made the graceless man more a liability than an asset.

Long followed the streams to the step pyramid and walked up the wide steps until he reached the main entrance. The arched glass doors opened into a chilled atrium, where the light passing through the waterfalls outside rippled and splashed over the dark marble floor.

Jewel-colored hummingbirds zipped past, chasing each other to the background music of a drowsy orchestral melody.

He felt he should applaud the theatrics, but restrained himself instead to a small half-smile.

The Lethes didn't sound like the kind of people who would enjoy his sense of humor.

A man in the Lethe colors of deep purple and slate gray approached him, white hair slicked back to an opalescent sheen. "May I help you, sir?"

"Doctor Malcolm Long. I have an appointment."

"Certainly, sir. If you'll please follow me."

He gestured to a bank of black lifts behind a discreet marble reception desk. The greeter stepped around and peered at a screen that Long had the good manners not to peek at.

Or at least not to get caught peeking at.

"You're a few minutes early, sir," the greeter said, glancing up at him with a moue of censure.

"My apologies. I have the day free if you would like me to wait." He must have rushed. And now I look too eager, he berated himself. On time was on time. Eager looked weak. Late was disrespectful. It was these little social mores that kept the culture of Descent afloat.

The greeter shook his head. "No, I apologize, sir. The computer recalculated the time based on the tram delay. You have arrived on schedule, but a few minutes later would have been acceptable as well. If you'll take lift number seven, sir, it will take you to your meeting room."

That wasn't much information to go on.

Today's invitation had come from Lethe Corp, but without a signature. It was one of the annoying habits of the business people on the first continent that they used to keep their rivals guessing. Not knowing who he was meeting with meant he couldn't study or prepare for the meeting, not unless he wanted to study the several hundred middle managers, division leads, and board members.

He stepped into the mirrored elevator and tried to avoid glancing at his reflection, afraid he'd catch himself glaring and remember what a bad idea it was to get caught up in the machinations of political fanatics.

The mirror image glared back anyway.

For good reason, too; he should have worn a touch of Lethe purple somewhere to show a willingness to work together. The dark gray suit with a white shirt was a little too neutral. Long jerked the edge of one cuff straighter, an expression of annoyance tugging at his lips. He suppressed that too. This was a stupid risk to take. But declining, he suspected, would have proven fatal.

The door to the lift opened to a long, wide room with a row of slit windows overlooking the city. The only furniture was a white stone desk, carved to look like it had grown out of the stone floor. The walls were lined with silent waterfalls that pooled around the edge of the room, filled with small green reeds that had either been genetically engineered for the poor lighting or were fake; he couldn't tell at this distance.

At the desk, a woman was silhouetted by the window light, her pale hair swept up into a coiling, sleek up-do and held in place by a pin with a dripping chain of amethysts that matched her silk shirt. She was framed by the jungle outside, a pale diamond in the city of jewels. The effect was stunning, albeit contrived.

Long waited in front of the lift for her to acknowledge him as a dark suspicion formed.

Several minutes crept by before the woman finished her work, turned off her screen and stood.

Recessed lights in the ceiling turned on as she moved, spotlighting Sonya

Lethe, the sole heir of the Lethe fortune.

Fear crawled down his spine with cold fingers.

This is what a fish feels like when it sees a shark. I always wondered.

"Doctor Long, please, come in," she said from behind the desk. "I'm delighted you could make time in your schedule to come to Kytan today."

"The delight is mine," he said, repeating the proper polite phrasing. "I've been looking for an excuse to come to Kytan."

"Wedding season," Sonya said with a slink of a smile. "Is there someone you were hoping to show the flowers to?"

"Much to my mother's dismay, there is not."

Sonya walked around her desk and perched on the front edge. "Yes, she is Nettie Amherst of the Northland Amhersts, isn't she?"

"The last of that line to bear the Amherst name, yes." Sonya had done her homework, both a threat and a show of strength. Or maybe she thought it put them on equal footing. After all, any schoolchild raised on Descent could name the Lethe heirs back to the first ship.

"Perhaps your future spouse will see fit to revive the name. Long is...." She pursed her lips as she looked him up and down in an appraising way. "...Perhaps a little generic?"

He let the insult pass with a smile. "My father says it's a dialect word from the Grizhjan System meaning 'dragon'. I make it a rule never to argue translations with a linguist."

Sonya laughed. It was a calculated move, the arch of her neck, the degree of her smile, the uplift of her breasts, all mathematically designed to hide the fact that the muscles around her eyes never moved.

She wasn't amused, she was manipulating him.

There were few things in the world that felt worse.

Long waited her out. Social graces did not require him to laugh along with her, so he didn't.

"Doctor Long, you look so grim. I do not like grim faces at business."

"Forgive me, Miss Lethe, I wasn't sure what response you anticipated. My name is not often a topic of conversation."

She smiled with an apologetic head tilt. "Engineers. You're always so delightfully focused, aren't you?"

"It's been mentioned before."

"Excellent." Sonya nodded. "Focus, I believe, is something this project needs. Please, take a seat."

She brushed her hand along a control set in the stone desk and a chair materialized to one side, perfectly set to give the occupant a view of both the city and Sonya at their best angles.

Long regarded the chair with quiet suspicion. It was a trap, that much was obvious, but he wasn't sure exactly what kind.

Days like this, he thought about throwing it all away and moving back to the islands.

But then he'd never be able to fly again. And flying again was the only reason he kept breathing. Everything else was lost to him, but maybe, one day, he could reclaim the sky.

"It's quite safe," Sonya assured him as she took her own seat behind the desk. "The matter transporter is something new our research and development team is working on. It could replace all travel one day."

All the more reason to hate it.

Aloud he said, "I'd heard of research along those lines, but I thought we were decades away from a breakthrough." Unless someone was getting tech from the space fleet that had landed on the third continent. He, like most people, wasn't privy to the fine details of the treaty the planetary representative had signed with them, but he felt certain the tech they'd brought with them was off limits.

"This can only move objects a few feet. But it is fun to bring a chair in from the closet at the touch of a button. There's an awe factor I appreciate." She sat back with a smug smile, the empress on her throne.

"I can imagine." He took a seat and dutifully surveyed the view of the city.

Sonya sat in the chair across from him, blonde hair framed by the shimmering blue flowers. "Tell me, Doctor Long, do you have your father's gift for languages?"

The question blindsided him and he let a frown slip. "No. Some, I suppose. I speak all the regional cants of the first and second continents and can read the Journals Of Discovery in the original Imperial Script, but that's a talent any well-educated person on Descent can boast of." Especially since the dialects only changed a handful of slang terms between all of them. Calling them languages was a bit of an insult to the idea of diversity, really.

"You claim to have no gift for languages, but you broke the hardest cipher we know while at university." She laughed. "What a shame everyone isn't as lacking in gifts."

"Ah," he said, shrugging one shoulder in dismissal. "Cryptography is a ghost from my misguided youth." And he hadn't broken the cipher alone. The key to the whole thing had been in an obscure text his classmate had found.

Technically, he should have credited her, but that would have required finding her after the move to Descent, and he hadn't had the resources. And she was unlikely to want to speak to him ever again anyway.

"I work exclusively in aeronautical science now. That was why I thought you'd called me in, to solve the fuel efficiency problems with the Koenig-360?" He let the opening dangle.

Sonya waved the comment aside. "Planes are relics. We can burn all the fuel we want. In a few years the new matter transporters will be the foundation of Lethe's transportation division. Let the Koenigs fly. This project is much more time sensitive." She held up a datcube, black and small enough to be concealed in his fist.

Long raised an eyebrow in question.

"This belonged to one of my employees. At the time of his death he had no heir, so the data became company property."

How convenient for Lethe.

"My techs have been able to decrypt a portion of the data on here, but the rest is beyond them. We've applied to other experts Lethe already has a working relationship with, but neither were able to decrypt it. Both experts mentioned you." She held the datcube out to him.

It was heavier than its size suggested. Someone had coated it in the anti-theft paint that had been popular for the past two years—which meant it wasn't too old to be recoverable—but on one side he felt an indentation, as if someone had pierced the cover with a fingernail.

It was all too easy to picture the previous owner holding this in a death grip in their final moments.

A sense of inevitable dread settled over him. It had been a mistake accepting the Lethe's offer. A mistake to be found on their radar at all. If he couldn't untangle himself—quickly— he would undoubtedly meet the same fate as the datcube's luckless owner.

"Have you considered the possibility that the information is corruptted?" Long asked. "I can guess which experts you would speak to, and who would recommend me, and there's very little I could do that they wouldn't have. There's no point in wasting your time if the data isn't salvageable."

Sonya shrugged. "I give it a twelve percent chance of being corrupted. It might be a keyed cypher, but the balance of probability says it's most likely an encryption."

"And the data?"

"Time sensitive only because of the employee's death."

A thin thread of hope appeared. "I realize it's tactless to ask, but is this datcube part of an ongoing investigation into that death? My clearance for several of my projects requires me to steer clear of the Jhandarmi and all local constabulary."

Please say yes.

Sonya gave him another calculated smile, this one undoubtedly meant to make her look innocent and charming. "The employee died because of a burst heart. The coroner ruled it death of natural causes."

The coroners of Descent would rule a stab wound death by natural causes if the right people asked. It was a line of thought he didn't dare to follow. "The best I can offer is to look at the encryption. Without seeing it I can't tell you anything more."

"Can you have a status report to me by the end of the week?" Sonya asked with a polite smile that said 'No' wasn't an acceptable answer.

Three days to unlock the datcube and analyze the contents was a tight timeline if he wanted to focus on his other work, but it was doable. He nodded. "A status report, but nothing more. Do you have a copy of the cube that I can take with me?"

Her lips slipped into an uncharacteristic grimace. "That is our only copy."

"Ah." He set it down on the desk between them. "That makes security problematic."

"Your lab is secure?" she asked.

"The research lab is, but the outer office is designed with client comfort in mind."

Sonya nodded in understanding. "The datcube will be sent by armed courier. Lethe can offer you the standard security fee for priority technology as well as a consultant fee." She twisted the screen on her desk he could see the numbers.

Standard fees, nothing that raised any red flags, although the whole affair seemed suspect.

"If you are able to decode the data, there will be a sizable bonus. Have you ever worked with Lethe before?"

"I've never had the pleasure." Just

as he'd never had the pleasure of being burned alive before. It was one of those little life-threatening things he'd made sure to avoid.

She pulled a paper contract from her desk drawer. "This is our consulting contract. While working on this project, you are not considered a Lethe employee and will not receive shares, benefits, or protections from Lethe. You will be paid commensurate to your skill level, and at the rate agreed. The contract terminates automatically after six weeks, unless both parties agree to extend the contract. Before, during, and after this project you are forbidden from disclosing the focus of the project with anyone other than your Lethe contact. Do you have any questions?"

Long looked over the paperwork. "Do you have the work of the previous groups that tried to decrypt this cube?"

"Would it be useful?" Sonya tilted her head.

"Knowing what they tried and what failed will save me time." And it would tell him who she had trusted.

Another small frown. "The other experts said they didn't want to be influenced by other people's processes." There was a hit of censure in her tone.

"We all approach work differently," he said. "I will probably look at it before reviewing their notes, but I don't feel the need to reinvent the wheel. Appearing like a genius to the world usually involves standing on the backs of geniuses who came before. It's how I did the decryption that I published in university."

Sonya gave a small nod, but he could see that she'd deducted a few points from the imaginary tally. "In that case, I'll make their work available to you. The records and a machine to process it on will arrive tomorrow. It goes without saying that everything stored on the computer becomes the property of Lethe after the contract is over."

"Of course." He made a mental note to scrub the machine for spyware and keep it away from his work lab and notes when it arrived. Lethe hadn't made their empire by playing fair.

Sonya stood up. "Then all is in order."

Following her lead, he stood too.

She posed, probably trying to look seductive. "I look forward to working with you, Doctor Long."

"And I look forward to working with you." As much as he looked forward to being eaten alive by ant lions. It was a trap, and the only way to escape was to move forward. If he could get Sonya the information maybe— just maybe—he'd escape with his life.

Keep reading! Head to
www.inkprintpress.com/lianabrooks/malik/change/
to buy your copy now!

ABOUT THE AUTHOR

LIANA BROOKS has long since left the mountains of Colorado for climates with better beaches. She still visits the mountains from time to time and enjoys seeing the snow in the high passes during the summer.

When she isn't traveling, Liana enjoys writing science fiction in every form, from sprawling space operas (*Fleet of Malik*) to the antics of a superhero family (*Heroes and Villains*).

You can learn more about her and her books at www.LianaBrooks.com.

INKLETS

Collect them all! Released on the 1st and 15th of each month.

INKLET
#055
Allure
AMY LAURENS

INKLET
#056
The LIES we
KNOW
LIANA BROOKS

DOUBLE
INKLET
#057
AFTERMATH
&
Fool Me Once
AMY LAURENS

INKLET
#058
Purity
An Age Of Unicorns Story
AMY LAURENS

INKLET
#059
Saved
AMY LAURENS

INKLET
#060
A Kiss is the
Secret
AMY LAURENS

INKLET
#061
A Changing Tides Story
Fire Bright
AMY LAURENS

INKLET
#062
Hades AND
Persephone
LIANA BROOKS

INKLET
#063
Just So Long
As You're Happy
AMY LAURENS

INKLET #064
Theft Of A Lifetime
LIANA BROOKS

INKLET #065
Shoe
AMY LAURENS

INKLET #066
Published AUTHOR
LIANA BROOKS

DOUBLE ISSUE
INKLET #067
The REMARKABLE INSIGHT of JELLYBEANS & Understanding
AMY LAURENS

INKLET #068
Desperate Measures
AMY LAURENS

INKLET #069
Rock-a-bye
LIANA BROOKS

INKLET #070
the Other Carly
AMY LAURENS

INKLET #071
B's By Bioluminescent Light
AMY LAURENS

INKLET #072
Even Villains Grant Wishes
A Heroes & Villains Story
LIANA BROOKS